Holly's BIKER

HOLIDAYS WITH THE BOSS

WALL STREET JOURNAL AND USA TODAY BESTSELLING AUTHOR

WINTER TRAVERS

For questions or comments about this book, please contact the author at winter@wintertravers.com

Also by Winter Travers

Devil's Knights Series
Loving Lo
Finding Cyn
Gravel's Road
Battling Troy
Gambler's Longshot
Keeping Meg
Fighting Demon
Unraveling Fayth
Forever Lo

Devil's Knights 2nd Gen
Passing the Torch
Riding the Line
Royal Mess
Changing Lanes
Bucking Tradition
Reining It In
Fractured Brotherhood

Skid Row Kings Series
DownShift
PowerShift
BangShift

Fallen Lords MC Series
Nickel
Pipe
Maniac

Wrecker
Boink
Clash
Freak
<u>Slayer</u>
<u>Brinks</u>
<u>Fallen Lords Christmas</u>

Kings of Vengeance MC
Drop a Gear and Disappear
Lean Into It
Knees in the Breeze
Midnight Wreckage
Thrill Seeker
Livin' on the Edge
Blacktop Freedom
Ride or Die

Powerhouse MA Series
Dropkick My Heart
Love on the Mat
Black Belt in Love
Black Belt Knockout

Nitro Crew Series
Burndown
Holeshot
Redlight
Shutdown

Royal Bastards MC: Sacramento, CA

Playboy
Six-Gun
Monk
Rebel
Barracuda
Jet
Jinx

VII Knights MC: Golden, CO Chapter
Iced

He Says Series
Wilder Presley Says He Loves Me
Charlie Beck Says I'm His (June 2023)

Sweet Love Novellas
Sweet Burn
Five Alarm Donuts

Stand Alone Novellas
Kissing the Bad Boy
Trapped with the Bad Boy
Daddin' Ain't Easy
Silas: A Scrooged Christmas
Wanting More
Mama Didn't Raise No Fool
Tangle My Tinsel
Mr. Motorcycle
Oral Communications
Coasting In
Holly's Biker

Table of Contents

*Thank you so much for picking up a copy of Holly's Biker.
It's been the year of getting out books that have been in my
head for years, finally out in the world.
I hope you enjoy this sweet novella about the grumpy boss
who finally wakes up and sees he's got the best thing right in
front of him.*

Happy reading.

Chapter One

Holly

"Can you get me the files on the Henderson bike?"

I cradled the phone to my ear and pulled open the file cabinet behind my desk. "Sure."

"It looks like we're about to go over the estimate, and I want to call them to see how much more they are willing to pay."

"Once I find it, I'll bring it to you."

Rook hung up without another word, and I turned to drop the phone back on the hook. "You're welcome, grumpy," I muttered.

Rook was always going over budget on his custom build bikes. Still, he always made the customers see that, in the end, a few extra thousand dollars made all the difference. I had told him he should keep the files for the customers he was working on in his office, but he never did.

Besides, why would he listen to me? I was just his secretary who knew every small detail about him and Rook on First Customs.

I knew this place wouldn't be able to run without me, but Rook did not think the same.

The man was a deadly combination of self-aware, cocky, and humility. Those three things did not go together under normal circumstances, but they worked together for Rook.

Though, if you asked me, that humility was the least of the three. His cockiness took over from time to time.

I shuffled through the files and grabbed the bulging Henderson one. It was stuffed with receipts, drawings, and even a few cocktail napkins that had notes scribbled on them.

"Come in," Rook called when I knocked on his door. I bumped the door with my hip and set the file on his desk.

"Is there anything else you need?" I asked.

Rook grabbed the file and laid it open. "What are we having for lunch?"

"It's Thursday."

Rook glanced up at me.

"You always have Crank's on Thursday." Rook was a man of habit. Monday was a ham and cheese with cole slaw from Jim's. Tuesday, it was shrimp tacos from Taco Palace. Wednesday, it was back to Jim's for a meatball sub. Thursday, sweet heat chicken wings with fries from Crank's. Friday, he finished the week with a beer-battered cod sandwich back at Jim's for the third time.

"I don't always have Crank's on Thursday," he insisted.

I folded my arms over my chest and tapped my foot. "So, you don't want chicken wings for lunch?"

Rook's eyes dropped back to the file. "I didn't say that," he mumbled.

I smirked and nodded to the file in front of him. "Let me know if you need anything else. Hopefully, Mrs. Henderson will loosen the purse strings, or you might be the owner of a custom V-Rod."

Rook scoffed. "You losing faith in me, Holly?" Rook leaned back in his chair and propped his arms above his head.

"I don't think you have ever had a customer like the Henderson's. Mitch may act like he wears the pants, but you damn well know Mindy is pulling up the zipper."

Rook tipped his head to the side. "That is a picture of the Hendersons I did not want in my head."

"Well," I laughed, "Can't take it back now."

Rook thinned his lips. "You can go now."

I bobbed my head slightly. "Yes, sir."

Rook growled, and I hightailed it out of his office before he could explode.

He hated when I called him sir. *Hated it.*

I shut his door and hurried back over to my desk. It was fun annoying Rook, but it could also be bad for my well-being. The man had a bit of an angry streak that I didn't want to turn on me.

Thankfully Rook stayed in his office, and I was spared his wrath about being called sir.

Forty-five minutes later, Rook's chicken wings and food for the rest of the shop arrived. Rook was set on what he ate during the week, and so was the shop. It was easier to order from the same places Rook wanted than to order from four or five different places. Rook provided lunch for each employee of Rook of First Customs, and thankfully they were all okay with just eating wherever the boss did.

I announced to the shop that lunch was here, and they descended upon the breakroom like a starving flock of seagulls.

I snagged Rook's Styrofoam container of chicken wings and knocked on his office door. Hopefully, he had cooled down from the whole sir thing earlier.

"What?" he shouted.

Uh, oh. Maybe Rook hadn't cooled down yet. I opened the door wide enough to stick my arm with the container. I was tempted just to set it on the floor and slowly back away. I shook the container and kept my body outside the door. "Lunch?" I called.

"Get your ass in here, Holly."

Not good.

I pushed open the door and stepped into his office

The mood here was not good.

Rook was behind his desk like before, but his mood had taken a nosedive, and a scowl had his lips turned down.

"Uh, is everything okay?" I asked. I held his lunch in both hands and wondered how mad he would be if I just tossed it at him and ran.

"Mindy Henderson," he hissed between clenched teeth.

Uh, oh. Things must not have gone well. "Did she loosen the purse strings?" I whispered.

Rook slammed his fist on the desk. "God dammit!"

I'm going to go out on a limb and assume that Mindy was not on board with Rook upping the price of the V-Rod.

I wore many hats around Rooks on First, and it seemed like I would be putting on my taming Rook hat.

I took a deep breath and stepped toward his desk. I set his lunch off to the side of a pile of papers and quirked my lips. "What did she say?" I asked.

"She'll pay the extra, but she wants some party to reveal the bike with all their fucking friends out on the show floor."

"Um, what?" I squeaked. That was a request I had never heard before. "I don't exactly follow what she's asking for."

"I don't fucking either," Rook raged. "I'm a goddamn biker who builds bikes, Holly. After the check clears, I throw the fucking keys at the customer, and then I move onto the next bike."

I was speechless.

Rook was not kidding when it came to giving the bike to his customers. The most I had ever seen him do was crack a few beers and make a little small talk.

Now Mindy wanted some huge reveal of the bike? "Uh, did you tell her no?" I asked.

Rook leveled his glare on me. "By the time I'm done with that bike, I'll have over fifty grand in it, and Mindy will pay me eighty thousand."

I knew the numbers. I just didn't know how much Rook didn't want to throw some reveal party. "Well, why don't we do a reveal? I mean, we have it here, I cater in some food, and boom, it's done."

Rook shook his head. "You haven't heard all of it yet, Holly." Rook spun towards the window and sighed heavily. "She wants a Christmas-themed party with all the fucking lights and tree bullshit."

"Really?"

"It's technically a present for Mitch, so Mindy wants to throw a party to show off to all of her friends how fucking rich she is. I fucking hate rich people."

I quirked my lips and held my tongue. Rook was rich. He technically hated himself then. The man owned and ran one of the most popular custom bike shops on the East Coast, and if he ever felt like taking off for a few weeks, he could and did.

I didn't know anyone else who could do that unless they were well off. Though, Rook was his own kind of rich.

Don't get me wrong; he did live in a large house at the foot of the Appalachian Mountains with a ten-car garage and a backyard oasis with a pool and hot tub. He also had more motorcycles than I could count, and he had a thing for classic trucks. He took his wealth and put it back into his shop and employees.

"But isn't Mitch the one you talked to about all the details for the bike? Seems kind of foolish to have a party to reveal it to him."

Rook spun back toward me. "Exactly, Holly. But we get back to them being rich who want to show off to all of their friends that they are rich."

"I wouldn't say all people who have money are like that," I reasoned.

"They aren't. These two just happen to be exactly what I hate."

I sighed and shrugged. "So, we throw up some decorations and have a party." I absolutely loved Christmas, and I wouldn't mind putting some decorations up around the shop. Rook had never been into Christmas and barely let me put a wreath on the front door.

"Mindy said she'll send over some photos for inspiration."

I cringed. "Wait, seriously?"

Rook nodded. "Yup."

"So you agreed to this?" I was damn surprised Rook was letting Mindy call the shots.

"She signed for the extra money for the bike. I can't turn my nose up to ninety-five-thousand dollars, Holly."

My jaw dropped, and I blinked rapidly. "Holy cow."

Rook nodded and pointed at me. "Yeah, now you get it. Whatever Mindy sends to me, I will forward it to you. She wants the reveal to happen in three weeks."

"Me?" I gasped. "Three weeks?" That didn't really give me much time.

"Yeah, you. You really think I am capable of planning some Christmas bike reveal?" Rook shook his head and laughed lightly. "This is going to be all you."

"I'm your secretary, Rook."

"And?"

"Well, and," I stammered, "I've never thrown a fancy party before."

"Look at the pictures she sends and duplicate them. You're one of the smartest people I know, Holly." His eyes connected with mine. "I know you can do this for me." He paused a beat. "Because if you don't, you're gonna have to buy that V-Rod."

"Wait, no, you can't be serious," I gasped.

Rook shrugged. "I guess knock this party out of the park, and you won't have to worry if I'm being serious or not." His phone dinged, and he swiped a few times. "I just forwarded the email to you."

"She already sent it?" What in the world? How did that woman already have the inspiration pictures she wanted for this party? It hadn't even been an hour since Rook had talked to her.

"Mindy probably already had this idea up her sleeve and figured she could squeeze the party out of me."

I pursed my lips. "Looks like she was right."

"Get out of my office, and let me eat in peace," he laughed. "I don't want to think about Mindy while I enjoy my lunch."

She was all I was going to think about while I ate.

I was going to add being an event planner to the long list of things I did around Rooks on First. "Wait."

Rook flipped back the lid to his food and looked up at me. "What?"

"What do I get if I pull this off?" I mean, if I was going to have to buy the V-Rod if I didn't make this happen, what would I get if it did happen?

"The satisfaction of knowing you did a job well done."

I rolled my eyes and flitted my hand at him. "Yeah, no. That's not going to be enough."

"Name your price."

I quirked my lips to the side and tapped my chin. "A seven-night cruise for two."

Rook tipped his head to the side. "For two?" he asked. "You managed to get a guy on the line?"

No. "Wouldn't you like to know?"

"I guess if I am going to buy two tickets for a cruise, I want to know who they are for."

"Why don't I make this party happen, and then we can get into the details of who is going on the cruise with me." That would give me three weeks to figure out whom I would bring along on the cruise. Which I would have to do while trying to plan a Christmas bike reveal party.

Rook laughed lightly. "Deal."

I flounced out of Rook's office and shut his door behind me.

I flopped down at my desk and pulled up my email. I opened the forward from Rook, and my jaw dropped.

Mindy had not sent a few photos over. She had sent over a bulleted list with specific things she wanted and thirty-seven photos.

Oh. My. God.

I had been rather confident about going on that seven-day cruise. Still, after reading over everything Mindy wanted, my confidence took a nose-dive.

Three weeks to turn Rooks of First into a winter wonderland.

I could totally do this.

Possibly.

My eyes darted to the words horse-drawn carriage.

I faceplanted on my desk and groaned.

I was screwed.

*

Chapter Two

Rook

Use the company credit card.

Duh.

Excuse me? I replied. I tapped my fingers on the desk and stared at my phone.

Sorry. I will use the company credit card. Thank you, sir.

I closed my eyes and took a deep breath. It was like Holly took joy in pushing my buttons. **Are you still out front?**

Clocked out for the day.

Lucky. And I meant she was lucky she wasn't here because she called me sir. I wasn't sir. Guys in suits and cushy office jobs were sir in my mind. I was Rook to anyone who talked to me.

See you in the morning, boss.

I dropped my phone on my desk and sighed. "Holly," I grumbled.

It was a good thing she was a damn good secretary; otherwise, she would have been out on her butt a long time ago.

But I knew if she weren't here, I would be shit out of luck with this whole Henderson Christmas party bike reveal.

I didn't know the first thing about throwing a Christmas party, but it seemed like it had only taken Holly a beat to get over the initial shock.

After lunch, I spent the afternoon in the shop and hadn't seen her before she left for the day. As much as I knew I needed to be in the office taking care of business and shit, I still just wanted to be in the shop building bikes and not dealing with nagging customers.

Holly helped with that.

Holly helped with a ton of shit I didn't want to deal with.

She was going to knock this party bullshit out of the park, and I honestly wasn't worried about it.

Well, maybe a little worried.

There was a lot of money on the line, and it was all riding on this Christmas party.

Holly could do it, though.

At least, time will tell.

*

Chapter Three

Holly

"Babe."

I stretched the shrink wrap over the leftover salmon and set it in the fridge. "Why are you babe-ing me?" I laughed.

Minx folded her arms over her chest and leaned against the counter. "Because I don't think you realize what you signed up for. You in danger, girl."

I grabbed a soda and bumped the fridge closed with my hip. "It's a Christmas party, Minx. I think I can handle this." I didn't think it was going to be easy, but I didn't think it was something I couldn't handle.

"Why don't you just hire an event planner? Jensen hired this wonderful woman last year for his company party, and she did an amazing job."

Minx was married to Jensen, and they lived next door. Jensen owned a commercial flooring company, and Minx was a stay-at-home wife. She hoped to change her title to stay-at-home mom, but that had yet to happen.

"Well, that does sound like the easy thing to do, but I know that Rook will not want me to spend one penny more than I have to. I plan on renting most everything and putting most of my budget into the food." All I had done today was stare at the email Mindy had sent and try not to freak out. I knew I was going to have to tackle the list one thing at a time, or I was going to be completely overwhelmed.

"That sounds like a good start, but I don't think you realize everything that goes into a party." Minx propped her hand on her hip. "How many people are invited?" she asked.

I popped the top on my soda and took a sip. "Well, the last count Mindy gave me was one hundred."

"*Babe*," Minx drawled. "That is a lot of people to invite to some bike reveal thing."

I shrugged. "Rook said the Hendersons are just wanting to flaunt the bike in front of their friends."

Minx shook her head. "No, sugar, they are flaunting their money."

I clicked my tongue. "That's what Rook said."

"You know, I still find it amusing that Rook complains about the rich when he is rich himself." Minx pushed off the counter and grabbed her sweater off the back of the kitchen chair. "I don't know many people who could sell a motorcycle for thousands upon thousands of dollars."

It was pretty amazing and, at times, unbelievable, but Rook did it. On the daily.

He had a waiting list of up to nine months for people that wanted to have a bike built by him.

"Well, if I don't pull off this party, I am going to be added to his roster of people who own a costly one of a king Rook custom." God, I hope that did not happen. I did not have eighty-thousand dollars lying around.

"Girl," Minx laughed, "as if that man would make you pay a penny for that bike. You and I both know that man could sell a Harley to a nun."

"I don't know. I think he might have met his match with the Hendersons."

"Whenever you say Hendersons, I think of the movie *Harry and the Hendersons* and assume that Mindy and Mitch look like John Lithgow and Melinda Dillon."

"Your ability to bring in old movies to every conversation is kind of scary, Minx." I never once thought of that old movie when Rook and I talked about the Hendersons.

Now I would.

"I better get back home. Jensen should be on the way home, and I have no idea what I am going to make him for dinner."

I nodded to the fridge. "Why don't you just take my leftovers?"

Minx smirked. "You sure?"

I rolled my eyes. "As if you didn't intentionally come over here, knowing full well that I can't cook for just one."

Minx opened the fridge and grabbed the container with salmon and asparagus. "So I am doing a favor for you. This would probably go bad before you ate it." She held up the container and shook it.

I wasn't sure about that, but I didn't mind if Minx and Jensen ate my leftovers. "You gonna try to pass it off as something you made?" I laughed.

Minx scoffed. "I wish, but you and I both know that Jensen knows I am not capable of making dinner, let alone salmon for dinner." Minx moved to the front door and glanced at me over her shoulder. "You know how I said you're in danger before?" she asked.

"Uh, yeah?" I laughed. Was she going to tell me again that I was out of my league with this party again?

"I mean with Rook, sugar."

Oh. I pointed my finger at her and shook my head. "Do not go there, Minx. I do not want to hear it tonight." Minx had this hair-brained idea that Rook was secretly in love with me, but he didn't know. Or he was denying it.

"Girl, I know that man has been holding out for a long time now, but I am telling you, there will be little Rooks running around here sooner rather than later." Minx had met Rook a handful of times when she visited me at work for lunch, but it wasn't like she sat down and had long talks with him. It was literally small talk between the two, but after the first time she met him, she acted like she knew his deepest, darkest secrets.

I scoffed and shook my head. "Right there, I know you are crazy because there is no way Rook would ever step foot in my apartment, let alone have kids with me and live here."

"Schematics, Holly. Mark my words, you and Rook will be Hook sooner rather than later."

I closed my eyes and shook my head. "You did not just ship Rook and me with a nickname."

"Sure did," Minx laughed. "You called me and Jensen, so now I'm calling you and Rook."

Oh, Minx. She was going to be so wrong. I flitted my hand at minx. "Go, take Jensen his dinner, and get any idea of little Rooks running around out of your head."

Minx tsked but stepped out the door. "I'll just watch quietly from the sidelines," she whispered. "And then gloat when I'm right." She winked and closed the door behind her.

I did not need that.

I had enough to deal with right now with the party. I did not need to go to work and wonder if Rook was into me and then start analyzing every glance, touch, or word.

No, thank you.

Tonight I was going to curl up on the couch to watch a cheesy Christmas movie, and tomorrow I was going to tackle the Hendersons bike reveal party.

I could totally do this.

I just had to keep telling myself that.

*

Chapter Four

Rook

"Rook to the office, please."

Holly's voice sounded around the body shop, and I growled.

I was elbow-deep in the V-Rod for the Henderson's, and I did not want to deal with office shit.

"Are we ignoring that?" Dane laughed.

I stood and wiped the grease off of my hands on a rag. "You really think Holly will let me ignore her?"

Dane shook his head. "Maybe for about five minutes, but longer than that? No."

He was right. The time it took me to wash my hands and up to the loft area where the offices were was about how long I had before Holly paged me again. "Keep working on the exhaust, and I'll be back down in ten minutes."

"Sure," Dane laughed.

I grumbled under my breath and headed up the stairs after washing my hands.

The layout of Rooks on First Customs was unique, but it worked well.

When you walked in the front door, you were immediately in the showroom where there were rare, one-of-a-kind bikes for sale. The showroom was massive at over ten thousand square feet. Behind the showroom was the shop where all of the magic happened. That was where you could normally find me as long as Holly wasn't calling me to the damn offices that were above the shop and showroom.

Holly's desk was by the door when you walked upstairs. Then mine was to the left, along with a breakroom, and on the right were two conference rooms that were used for customer consultations.

"Can we make this quick?" I asked as I opened the door.

Holly was behind her desk with tons of papers in front of her.

"There is a way to make this quick, but I really doubt that is the way it is going to go."

I didn't like the sound of that.

"What?" I laughed. "Do we have to add some camels and llamas for the Henderson bike reveal?" I looked at the email Mindy sent over yesterday. It was all ridiculous bullshit. I had gotten to the third bullet and stopped reading. Twinkle lights were not something I was interested in.

"Shh." Holly pressed her finger to her lips. "Mindy might hear that and want it." Her eyes darted from side to side, and she smiled mischievously.

I moved behind Holly's desk and looked down at the papers on her desk. "What is all of this stuff?"

Holly tipped her head to the side and looked up at me. "This is just a little bit of what Mindy has on her list of things she wants for the reveal."

"How long does she think the party is going to be?" I growled. "Honestly, what the hell is this woman thinking? It's a damn motorcycle, not a baby or something."

Holly scoffed. "I don't think people do baby showers as extravagant as Mindy wants this to be." She grabbed a piece of paper and read from it. "If possible, we would like there to be elves as waiters. They don't need to be short, just dressed in green and red jumpers with pointy ears." She tossed the paper on the desk and sighed. "We need to discuss your budget for this party."

"Small."

"Rook." Holly glared and quirked her lips. "I'm being serious here."

"And so am I." I stepped to the side and rested my hip against her desk. "I don't want to pay a dime for this party."

Holly wheeled her chair back a bit and leaned back. "Then why did you agree to do it?"

I shrugged and folded my arms over my chest. "Because it's probably going to be easier throw this party than to find another buyer for this bike." V-Rod Mitch wanted was damn nice, but we were building to exactly what he wanted. Could I sell it to someone else? Sure, but it would take time to find the right buyer. I had the right buyer in Mitch and didn't want to lose him.

"You might not say that when I tell you how much just the decorations alone are going to cost." Holly tapped her fingers on the armrest of her chair. "She wants twenty-five trees, Rook. One for each year they've been married, and they all need to be decorated differently."

"How the hell do you decorate twenty-five trees differently?" I growled. "Throw some damn lights on the things, and then call it done."

"I wish this was that easy." Holly grabbed one of the papers on her desk. "Mindy had some more papers sent over."

I grabbed the paper and glared at it. "She had then sent over?" I spat. "Who on the hell does that when she can just email the shit?"

"Someone with too much money and too much time on their hands?"

I scanned over the paper, and my scowl grew. "Does she really think anyone is going to care that one of the trees is decorated in blue and silver because it was their wedding colors?" "I'll take care of it." I balled up the paper and tossed it in the trash.

"You'll take care of it?" Holly laughed. "What does that mean?"

"It means take all of this shit that she's sending over as suggestions. All I agreed to is having a Christmas-themed bike reveal. You do it however you want to."

"But what about all the things Mindy wants?"

I shook my head and pushed off her desk. "If she wants the party this way or that way, she can plan and pay for it. She wants the bike revel here; then she is going to get whatever we give her."

"We?" Holly asked. "Does that mean you are going to help me?"

I wrinkled my nose. "Uh, well, I'll help with setting everything up." I nodded toward the shop. "And you know everyone else will help."

"And I have your blessing to do it how I want to?" she asked.

"Within reason, Holly."

"Does that mean I have a budget?" she winced.

I nodded. "Yeah, babe. Keep it under ten grand." That seemed like way more than she would need. At least, I hoped it was.

"Do you want a sit-down meal or just some little finger foods? Open bar or cash bar?"

"Finger foods and open bar. I'm raising my middle finger to Mindy by not doing the party up the way she wants, but we're still gonna have booze flowing."

"Can't take the biker out of the man," Holly mumbled.

"What was that?" I asked.

Holly plastered a smile on his lips. "Oh, nothing."

"Ain't nothing wrong with being a biker, sugar. Bikers are what keep this place running."

Holly swiveled toward her desk. "You are not wrong about that, Rook. Maybe I'll see about getting myself one of the bikers that walk through the door."

Her words hit me like a punch to the gut.

Holly had never joked or even talked about catching a biker. Hell, she never spoke about catching anyone. Not in the five years that she had worked for me.

"None of them are good enough for you, Holly."

Her eyes darted to me and then back to her computer. "I don't know about that, Rook. If those guys treated me half as good as they treat their bikes, I would be a happy woman."

I grunted and reached for the rest of the papers on her desk. I wasn't interested in talking about this. "Throw these away," I growled.

Holly tried to knock my hands away. "No, no," she protested. "I want to keep them because there are some good ideas."

"Where in the hell are you going to put twenty-five trees, Holly?" I grabbed some of the papers and lifted them over my head. "Just do the party the way you want to. I'll handle Mindy if she gets rowdy about things not going her way." I was sort of looking forward to being able to put that damn woman in her place. God knew Mitch let her walk all over him, but she wasn't going to be that way with me.

"Rook," Holly cried. She jumped up and tried to grab the papers but lost her balance and fell into me. She pressed her hand on my chest, and I wrapped my arm around her waist.

"Simmer, sugar," I whispered. I kept my arm above my head and steadied her against me. Her eyes connected with mine, and her breath hitched.

"Uh, I…" she stammered. "I'm not going to fall."

"That's because I'm holding you." She stepped back, and I loosened my arm around her waist but didn't let her go. "You don't need these papers. You don't have to do a damn thing Mindy wants."

"I know," she whispered.

"Do whatever you want. I know you love Christmas." Holly always bugged me to decorate the show and showroom more for the holiday, but I always resisted. This was her chance to finally do what she always wanted.

"I do, but I know you don't."

I shrugged. "Not that I don't, it's just…." I wasn't sure what it was.

"You just don't like Christmas," she laughed.

I reached up and hooked my finger under her chin. "I've just never had someone to share it with.

What's the point of having something if you don't have anyone to share it with?"

I felt a shiver run through her body and bit her bottom lip. "You have family, don't you?" she asked.

"Yeah, a sister in California, and my parents are off RVing around the country." We weren't exactly a close family, and being all the way across the country didn't help to make us closer.

"Well," Holly sighed, "You have all of the guys in the shop and the showroom. You can get festive for them."

"And you?" I asked softly.

"I mean, well," she bristled. "I was including me in with them."

I trailed my fingers across her cheek. "Well, I wasn't"

"Whatever you want," she whispered.

"Rook to the showroom," Dane's voice crackled over the intercom.

Jesus.

Holly blinked rapidly and pulled out of my arms. "You, uh, better go see what that is about. Maybe you've got another big client on the line."

I dropped the papers on her desk and straightened. "Well, that may be, but they're gonna have to wait a few months before they get their own bike reveal."

Holly laughed nervously and tucked a stray strand of hair behind her ear. "Maybe you can offer the bike reveal as an extra package."

"Also, for an extra charge," I grumbled.

"Yes," Holly laughed. "I think the Henderson bike will be a learning lesson for us all. Stay on budget, and ensure you get enough money for the reveal party if they want one."

"A twenty-four pack of beer and a pat on the shoulder is pretty much all they're going to get from me if you're not in charge of the reveals, sugar. You wanna add that package; you're gonna be the one selling it."

Holly rolled her eyes. "You never know, Rook. This party could be huge for Rooks on First. You know there are going to be people attending who have money just burning a hole in their pockets."

"Rook to the showroom, "Dane called again.

Holly held in her finger. "Before you run off, I need to know if you were serious about the budget."

"Ten grand. I can write it off since it's for the business."

Holly nodded and smiled. "You may run along, then. That was really all I needed when I called you."

I tipped my head and smirked. "Just wanting to know how much of my money you can spend."

Holly shrugged. "I was just going to spend what I wanted and ask for forgiveness later, but I thought getting a number from you was more professional."

"You made the right choice, sugar." I opened the door to the showroom and glanced back at Holly. "And I know whatever choices you make for the party are going to be the right ones, too."

"Just keep Mindy off my back," she warned. "You told me you would handle her."

I nodded and jogged down the steps. All I was going to do with Mindy was ignore her. She could send party instructions and ideas by fucking pigeon, and I wouldn't care.

Holly was in charge of the party. End of story.

I reached the bottom of the stairs and glanced back up at the offices.

But the way my heart stuttered when Holly mentioned finding a biker of her own? I was pretty sure that was the beginning of a story I didn't see coming.

Holly had worked for me for five years, and I had always viewed her from an employee perspective.

Sure, I wasn't blind and knew she was beautiful, but I never crossed the line.

Until now, when crossing the line seemed like the right and only thing to do.

The one thing I knew for sure was that Holly would not hook up with one of the bikers who walked through the doors of Rooks.

Hell no.

*

Chapter Five

Holly

"And that is the cost for twelve?"

"Yeah, we're giving you a quantity discount. Never had anyone want to buy twelve Christmas trees," the man on the other end of the phone laughed.

I had spent the rest of my morning looking for places to rent Christmas trees from but had discovered it would be cheaper in the long run if we just bought them outright and stored them. Heck, I was maybe even considering leaving a couple up and decorating them for each holiday.

"I can be there in half an hour to pick them up." I wrote the price of the trees on a notepad and circled it. "And what is your name?" I asked.

"Chuck, ma'am. I'll start putting them aside for you."

I hung up and pumped my fist in the air.
Heck yeah.
Some people skydive or climb mountains for a thrill. Me? Getting a good deal and saving money gave me a thrill even when it wasn't even my own money I was saving.

I set up the office calls to be transferred to my cell phone, then grabbed my keys, and jogged down the steps to the shop.

"Where are you going?" Rook called. He was standing by a bike that was scattered around him in a million pieces.

"I'm on a mission," I laughed. "Calls are being forwarded to my phone, and I should be back in an hour if everything goes as planned."

"Where the heck are you going?" Dane asked. He was crouched next to Rook and had what looked like a piece of exhaust pipe in his hand.

"I'm off to see a man about a few trees."

"Oh, god," Rook moaned. "Please tell me you are not getting all those trees that Mindy wanted."

I lifted both hands and weighed them up and down. "Kind of, but on a smaller scale." I had liked the idea of having various trees, but just not such a considerable number. I stopped in my tracks and looked down at my keys. "Shoot," I gasped.

"What?" Rook called. He made his way over to me and looked at my keys. "Something wrong?"

I pursed my lips and tipped my head back. "How busy are you right now?" I could probably fit two of the trees in my car, which meant it was going to take me six trips back and forth to get all the trees.

"What the heck do you got going on, sugar?" Rook laughed.

I plastered a huge smile on my face. "Feel like taking a little field trip with me?"

"Field trips haven't been part of my vocabulary for years."

I slapped my hand on his arm. "Well, it looks like today that changes. I need you, the big truck, and the trailer."

"And this is why you should have listened to me when I tried to show you how to drive the truck with the trailer."

"Just like a field trip is not in your vocabulary, Rook, a truck with a trailer is not in mine."

Rook growled, but he didn't tell me to get lost.

"Please?" I pleaded. I batted my eyes at him and clasped my hands in front of me. "For me?"

"God dammit," Rook grumbled. "Dane," he shouted. "I'll be back. Keep working on the bike, and let me know if the exhaust works."

Dane saluted. "You got it, boss."

Rook grabbed my arm and steered me toward the back door. He grabbed the keys to the shop truck by the back door and pushed open the door.

"Hop in." He guided me over to the shop truck and opened the passenger door.

"How the heck am I supposed to get in there?" I asked. The floor of the truck was almost at chest height, and I was going to need a running start to maybe be able to project myself inside.

Rook pointed to the step. "Put your foot there, and I'll do the rest."

I looked up at him. "Excuse me?"

Rook's eyes narrowed. "You want me to take you to get the trees or not?" he asked.

I held up my hands. "Fine, fine. You call the shots, sir." I lifted my left foot and rested it on the step. "Like this?"

Rook grunted and swung me up into the truck with zero effort. It was like he had tossed a feather into the truck, not my two-hundred-pound body.

"Jesus," I gasped. I had a whole new perspective from up here. For once, I was the one looking down at Rook.

He tipped his head back, and his eyes connected with mine. "You're just gonna act like you didn't just call m sir?" he asked.

I tipped my head to the side and laughed. "I didn't even realize I had."

Rook grunted. "Sure." He slammed my door shut and stalked around the front of the truck. He hopped into the driver's seat and cranked up the truck.

"Are you mad?" I asked over the loud diesel engine.

Rook shook his head and drove around the side of the building. He backed up to the large trailer and jumped out to hook it up.

I watched him out of my door mirror and admired the way his muscles flexed and moved as he cranked the trailer down. He hooked it to the hitch and then jumped back into the truck.

"Where are we headed?" he asked.

I licked my lips and tried to get my beating heart under control. "Uh, the Yard All on the other side of town. Chuck said he would put the trees aside for me."

"Chuck?" Rook grunted.

I quirked my eyebrow. "Um, yes. Chuck."

Rook grunted but didn't say anything else.

We drove to Yard All in silence, but my head was racing with many thoughts.

Why was he mad at me? Did he really care who the heck Chuck was? He easily could have told Dane to drive me to Yard All. Why didn't he?

Why was I suddenly noticing, well, everything about Rook?

I would have had to be blind and deaf not to know the man was handsome. But that had never affected me before.

Now? Now I was noticing more than ever. And why did I care if he was mad at me? Annoying Rook was one of my favorite things to do, and not I was worried I had called him sir one too many times.

We pulled into the parking lot of Yard All and parked in the back.

I licked my lips and turned to Rook. "Uh, I kind of want to look at what else they have here. Is that okay?" I asked.

Rook grunted and put the truck keys in his pocket. "Whatever you want."

I raised my eyebrows. "Seriously?"

Rook shrugged. We're here, and we have the trailer and truck. Get whatever the heck you need."

Decoration shopping with Rook.

That was something I never thought I would do.

"You can stay in the truck if you want." I could totally look around and grab things by myself.

Rook shook his head and hopped out of the truck.

"Okay then," I muttered. I grabbed my purse and hitched it over my shoulder. Rook opened my door before I could get my hand on the handle. He stood in front of me, effortlessly turned me in my seat, and lowered me to the pavement with his hands at my waist.

"Uh, thank you," I whispered. I hadn't even had time to wonder how I was going to get down before Rook was there.

"Anything for you."

There were those words again.

Rook had never spoken them to me before today, and I liked them. "Let's see if you're still saying that after we get done here."

I had looked online at all the things Yard All had, and I was confident I was going to put a big dent in my list of decorations.

Rook turned toward the store and held his arm out to me. I hooked my arm through his and smiled wide.

I wasn't sure what the heck was going on, but I liked it.

God help me; I liked being with Rook.

*

Chapter Six

Rook

"That it?" I parked another full cart by the registers.

Holly quirked her lips and surveyed the three full carts. "I hope so."

One whole cart was loaded down with strings of lights, pine garland, and twelve tree skirts. The other two carts were ornaments.

Honestly. The two carts were overflowing with a fuck ton of ornaments. And Holly wasn't even sure that was going to be enough.

We easily had close to two grand between the three carts and had another fifteen hundred for the trees that were waiting outside for us.

"I guess the one good thing about all of this stuff is that we can use it every year, right?" I was trying to find the Brightside of spending all this money on Christmas decorations. Thank god it was all write-offs.

Holly smiled brightly. "Yes, totally! And, we can leave a couple of the trees up and decorate them for different holidays."

I chuckled and shook my head. "Now, you might be asking for too much, sugar."

We had been in the store for close to an hour, and it was another half an hour until we were checked out and loaded up.

Normally the truck was used to pick up and haul motorcycles around, but now it was hauling Christmas shit. The truck's bed was full of ornaments, lights, and other shit Holly had tossed in the cart. The trailer had twelve large boxes stacked on it that held the twelve trees Holly had some type of vision for.

Holly opened her door, and I yelled for her to wait for me.

"No, no," she called. "I can get up here myself." She managed to get her foot on the running board and hoist herself up, but then she didn't know how to swing herself in. "Little help," she called.

I managed to get to her before her hands slipped, and she fell right into my arms.

"Sugar," I grunted.

She huffed, and her eyes were bugged out. "I thought I had it," she whispered.

"Almost," I chuckled. "Maybe next time you should wait for me."

"But then I won't end up in your arms, right?" Holly's eyes bugged out, and she slapped her hand over her mouth. "I didn't just say that," she muttered.

She had, and I liked the way she thought. "You don't have to throw yourself around to get into my arms, sugar." And now I had just said that.

"Oh, uh," she gasped. "Good to know," she squeaked.

That might have crossed the line, but from where I was standing right now, the other side of the line looked pretty fucking good.

I lifted her into the truck and tucked her in safely. "See, you just needed to wait for me, sugar."

"My biker in worn leathers," she sighed jokingly.

I laughed softly and closed her door.

This was all fucking new when it came to Holly and me.

Sure, we were friendly with each other, but we were flirting with, well, flirting.

I didn't know what this meant for us, but I was ready to find out where we were headed.

The last time I had been with a woman was over a year ago. I dated on and off, but it was never with the same woman.

Sure, I had the opportunity to hook up pretty much whenever I wanted, but I was getting to the age where a random fuck wasn't what I wanted anymore.

Maybe what I needed and wanted was right underneath my nose.

Maybe that was Holly.

*

Chapter Seven

Holly

"Tell me again."

I shook my head and downed the last of my wine.

"Holly," Minx whined. "You have to tell what happened next."

"Nothing," I sighed. "Nothing happened. Rook got in the truck, we drove back to the shop, and then we unloaded everything." I wasn't sure what I wanted to happen, but I knew it was more than what had happened.

Did I think Rook would express his undying love for me in front of the whole shop? No, of course not. But did I wish he wouldn't have put me in the truck so quickly and maybe tried to kiss me? Uh, yeah.

Never did I wonder what it would be like to kiss Rook, but now it was all I could think about.

And Minx wasn't helping me to get the thought out of my head.

"Min," Jensen called. "Would you leave her alone? She's told the story three times already."

Minx stuck her tongue out in the direction of Jensen, who was sitting in the living room.

"I know you just stuck your tongue out at me," Jensen called.

Minx pursed her lips and growled. "How does he do that?"

"He's got eyes in the back of his head?" I suggested.

'Or I just know my wife," Jensen called. "And hopefully, my wife knows I am ready to go home."

Minx pouted out her lips. "Already?" she asked. "We just got done with dinner. I'm sure Holly has dessert."

"I'm only interested in your dessert, Minx."

"Oh god," I groaned. "I think it's time for you two to go home," I laughed. "I don't want to see Jensen have his dessert."

"Please," Minx grumbled. "By the time he gets his dessert, he'll be passed out before I can even take the shrink wrap off."

A very vivid picture of Minx wrapped in shrink wrap flashed in my head. "Oh no," I gasped.

"Oh yes," Jensen called. "I'll get the shrink wrap ready, babe." Jensen jumped over the back of the couch and grabbed his coat off the back of the kitchen chair. "Thanks for dinner, Holly. It was just as good as the salmon the other night." He slipped out the door but kept it open.

"Girl, you better get your butt home if you don't want him falling asleep on you."

Minx laughed and grabbed the container with leftovers off the counter. "Keep me posted on what Rook does next," she called. "I might even pop into Rook's while I run errands next week. I'd love to see what you have going for the party."

"Nothing right now other than a lot of boxes. You shouldn't come."

Minx shook her head. "One week, Holly. I'm giving you one week, and then I'm there."

"You're crazy. I might just be making a mountain out of a molehill about the whole truck thing with Rook." I wasn't, but I didn't need Minx coming into work and hoping to get a show from Rook and me.

Minx wrinkled her nose. "If anything, you're not making a big enough deal about it. Let that man swoop you off your feet again, Holly, and I guarantee it will end way better than it did this time." She waved her fingers at me and slipped out the door.

I swung it shut behind her and sighed.

Jesus.

How did I go from having nothing but a neutral feeling for Rook to wondering what it was like to kiss him and maybe orchestrating how to make it happen?

"Focus, Holly," I hissed.

The man was my boss, and he was way out of my league.

The man was a self-made millionaire who could have any woman he wanted. Hell, I had seen the women he had, and I didn't even compare to them.

I was just Holly, Rook's mousy secretary.

I needed to get this afternoon out of my head and focus on work.

That was it.

No Rook, just work.

Except that was hard since Rook was part of my work, and I saw him all the time.

I took a deep breath and stood straight.

But I could do it.

I was Rook's secretary, and that was it.

I think.

*

Chapter Eight

Rook

I had to kiss her.
There was no other option.
I just had to find the right time.
Holly was going to be mine.

*

Chapter Nine

Holly

Putting together one tree? Easy.

Putting together twelve and then moving them to where you want them? Hard.

Not to mention I also had a vision of one of the trees being suspended from the loft by the offices, which was level three hard.

Hell, this whole party was turning out to be level three hard.

It had been four days since Rook, and I had got the trees and decorations from Yard All, and I wasn't very far into my plan of turning Rooks into a biker winter wonderland.

"Girl," Megan from the showroom called. "We're all heading out. I'm going to lock the front door, yeah?"

I blew a stray strand of hair out of my face and plastered a smile on my lips. "Sounds good! Have a good night." Man, I wished I was heading home. I needed to get at least half of these trees assembled and staged around the showroom.

I was two weeks away from the party, and I did not want to wait until the last minute to get all of this done. Rook was going to have to deal with being festive for the next two weeks.

"And I'll talk to my dad tonight and see if he's up for adding some Santa magic to the party." Megan laughed and hitched her purse over her shoulder. "Once I tell him it's for Rook, I know he'll be all in."

Megan's dad was a regular around Rooks, who was also a dead ringer for Santa but with a biker flare. I had a vision of biker Santa mingling among the guest and handing out little packages with little trinkets or even gift cards for Rooks merchandise.

"Tell him there will be all the appetizers he can eat and an open bar."

Megan gave me a small salute. "Then I can guarantee he will be there. Don't work too hard, Holly." Megan headed back into the showroom, and I listened for the last sound of everyone leaving.

"And then there was one."

My heart leaped, and I clutched my hand to my chest. "My god, Rook," I gasped.

Rook stood on the landing to the offices with a smug smile and leaned against the railing. "Forget I was here, sugar?"

Well, yes. The last I had seen of Rook, he was headed out the large shop door on his motorcycle.

Now he was looming over me while I struggled to put Christmas trees together. "I thought you were gone for the day."

He shook his head. "Just had a few errands to run. What are you up to?"

I held up one of the branches that needed to be stuffed into the frame of the tree. "Oh, you know, just lounging around and putting some trees together."

"You need some help?" he asked.

"I do, but I really doubt tree assembly is something you want to be doing on a Tuesday night."

Rook shrugged. "Not much else to do." He nodded to me. "Why don't you order some dinner, and I can help you get those done."

"You don't have to," I insisted. I was the one who wanted to have twelve Christmas trees, so I was aware that I needed to be the one to make it happen. I just wish I had looked a little closer at the trees before I bought them. I really thought they were going to be three sections to stack on top of each other, and then I was done.

Nope.

Every branch needed to be stuck into the tall frame of the tree. Not easy.

"I've been watching you struggle for the past ten minutes, Holly. I can say with confidence you need help."

I rolled my eyes but conceded. "Fine, you're right. I do need help." And I was getting hungry. I had ordered lunch for Rook and the shop today but didn't get anything for myself because I had been busy on the phone trying to find a caterer for most of the afternoon. "And we get what I want for dinner," I bargained. I wasn't too sure how much help Rook was going to be, so I might as well get something I wanted for dinner if he was going to be a pain.

Putting a custom bike together was something Rook could do in his sleep, and he loved it. I wasn't too sure he was going to love putting together trees.

Rook slowly walked down the stairs, and I kept my eyes on him.

He really was a sight to be seen.

He had a rough, bad boy façade to him that instantly drew your attention. Once he had your attention, you could get lost in his mossy green eyes and perfectly sculpted body. He typically wore plain t-shirts and jeans, but there was just something about how they fit his body. It was like he had all his clothes tailored to his body, but I knew Rook wouldn't waste money on that.

The man just looked good no matter what.

"And what is it you want?"

I blinked rapidly and shook my head. "Uh, what?" I mumbled.

"For dinner, Holly. What is it you want for dinner?"

Jesus. I thought for a second there Rook was able to read my mind. "Indian," I croaked. "I was going to order Indian."

Rook shrugged. "Never had it, but I guess I can give it a try."

"I think you'll like it." I tucked my hair behind my ear and ripped my eyes from Rook. I needed to stop staring at the man and focus on anything else. *Anything else.* "I can get you some butter chicken or tandoori chicken."

Rook grimaced. "Butter chicken?" he grunted.

"It's not what it sounds like," I giggled. "I promise you'll like it." I had been pretty much feeding Rook for the past five years and knew what he did and didn't like when it came to food. "There is more to it than just butter and chicken."

Rook sighed. "I guess I'll trust you, Holly. You haven't steered me wrong in the five years I've known you."

I pulled out my phone and pulled up the menu to order online.

"They deliver?" he asked.

"Most places do, Rook. And if they don't, I can normally order it through a delivery app."

Rook shook his head and surveyed the pieces of tree strewn around me. "I'm only thirty-seven, Holly, but sometimes I feel a hell of a lot older. You lost me at delivery app."

I glanced up at him and rolled my eyes. "You don't know what I'm talking about because I pretty much do everything for you, Rook. I even have your groceries delivered weekly to you."

"Hey," Rook laughed. "In my defense, you have to admit it is confusing to have your doorbell ring, and when you open the door, your groceries are there."

I snorted and added a few different Indian dishes to my order for Rook to try. "That still has to be the funniest phone call I have ever gotten." I dropped my voice an octave. "Holly, my doorbell just rang, and when I opened the door, there was food just sitting on my porch. What do I do?" I tossed my head back and laughed my butt off.

"Ha, ha," Rook grumbled.

"I even told you your groceries were going to be delivered."

Rook crouched down and grabbed one of the branches of the tree. "You gonna keep laughing or order dinner?" he growled.

"Both," I laughed. I finished the order for food and submitted the order. "There," I sighed. "It should be here in about half an hour. Maybe we can get one of these trees done by then."

Each branch was lettered, and we needed to put the z's in the bottom holes and work our way up the frame through the alphabet.

Each letter had seven branches, which meant we had over one hundred and fifty branches to put in each tree. Granted, things went quickly by the time we got to the top.

"Why don't you work on sorting out the branches, and I'll start sticking them in."

"You literally looked at this for ten seconds, and you already know what to do?"

Rook shrugged. "I'm good at putting things together."

"Yeah," I laughed, "but I didn't know that also meant Christmas trees."

When the food arrived, Rook was putting the last branches on the tree, and I was opening the next box.

I grabbed the food from the driver and set everything out in the showroom on the service desk.

"Do you want me to make you a plate?" I called to Rook. I had propped open the doors between the shop and showroom and glimpsed Rook, sticking the last branch in.

"Sure," Rook called. "Not like I'm going to know what any of it is."

I rolled my eyes and worked on filling a plate for him.

I heard Rook move into the bathroom and turn on the water. "That tree is a pain in the ass, Holly. Why in the hell did you get it?"

I laughed and grabbed a fork for Rook. "Because I'm trying to do all of this within the budget you gave me, Rook. The less I spend on decorations, the more I can put into the food."

Rook walked into the showroom and grabbed the plate from me. "I thought we were just doing appetizers?"

I grabbed a plate for myself and put a large scoop of rice on it. "We are, but it's not like appetizers are cheap just because they are small."

"Should be," Rook grumbled. He ate a forkful of butter chicken and chewed thoughtfully.

"Good?" I asked.

Rook didn't answer and took another bit.

It seemed like he was trying to figure out whether he liked it.

"What's the name of this place?" he asked.

I nodded to the empty bag I had set next to the food. "Surly Kabob."

"They cater?" Rook asked.

"Uh, well, I'm not really sure. Why?"

Rook took another bit, and this time he let out a moan. "Because that shit is good, Holly. I don't know what the hell I'm eating, but we need this at the party."

I had hoped that Rook would like it, but I didn't know he was going to like it so much that he would want it at the party. "Are you serious?"

Rook nodded. "Yeah. I'm paying for the party, so I should be able to say what food we eat, right?"

I mean, he wasn't wrong. "I can call tomorrow and see if they cater." Or if they could just make a butt load of butter chicken, and I could figure out how to serve it. I wasn't too sure that Mindy would be down with butter chicken, but whatever. "You are collecting the money for the bike before the party, right?"

Rook smirked and nodded. "Fuck yeah, sugar. No way in hell I will let any of Mindy's snobby friends into Rooks without that check clearing the bank first."

"In that case, I will for sure call Surly Kabob tomorrow and see if they can cater the whole party." Indian cuisine wasn't what Mindy wanted, but I guess in the end, if it tasted good, they would eat it. "I do have the desserts planned, so don't go and change that on me," I teased.

Rook raised his eyebrows. "Dessert?"

Rook had a major sweet tooth, and I knew the mini pies, platters of festive cookies, and sugar plum bread pudding cups were going to be perfect. "Like you didn't know we would have dessert at the party."

He winked and licked sauce off his finger. "I wasn't worried about it since you're in charge. You know what I liked."

Jesus. It was good that I had been blind to Rook's charms and looks for the past five years. I never would have gotten anything done if I hadn't had blinders on. "Yeah," I whispered.

"You okay?" Rook asked, concerned.

I pasted a smile on my face. "Yeah, I must have swallowed wrong."

I managed to eat the rest of my dinner without making a fool of myself or yelling out to Rook how handsome he was.

I needed to get a handle on my feelings and figure out what I wanted. Minx telling me all the time that Rook was secretly in love with me was messing with my head.

Or, maybe he was into me.

I was a strong, independent woman who, under normal circumstances, had no problem saying what I wanted and felt. Granted, Rook had never been a part of those scenarios.

Rook and I were back in the shop with another tree scattered around us. I was seriously considering returning all these trees. They were a pain in the ass.

"Where are you planning on putting all of these trees?" Rook asked.

I blew a piece of hair out of my face and fell back on my butt. "Here, there, everywhere," I laughed. "You know people are going to want to see where all of the magic happens, so I plan to do some decorating out here."

"Holly," Rook groaned. "You are not going to shoot glitter and shit all over the shop. We have to work here."

I rolled my eyes and shook my head. "I'm not shooting glitter anywhere, and it's not gonna hurt your workflow to have a couple of trees in here."

Rook grunted.

"Two there." I pointed to the door connecting the shop and showroom. "One in between each bay door." I quirked my lips and let my crazy idea out. "And then I wanted to put one at the top of the stairs but have it floating above everyone."

"Floating above everyone?" Rook repeated slowly. "Did you check to make sure our insurance is up to date?"

"Well, no, but I know it is." I stood and moved to the foot of the stairs. "I think we can do it with some zip ties."

"And some wishful fucking thinking," Rook laughed. "Was this one of Mindy's fucking ideas?" Rook moved beside me and glared at the stairs.

My cheeks heated, and I shrugged. "Uh, well, not really. It was my idea. I thought it would be something neat."

Rook hmphed. "Maybe the guys and I can rig something up."

My eyes snapped to Rook. "Really?" I knew it was a crazy idea, but I really wanted to make it happen.

"You want it? I'll make it happen."

Simple as that. "You must be in a good mood. Maybe I should ask for something else, too." I tapped my finger on my chin and quirked my lips.

"I'm always in a good mood, Holly."

"Ha!" I burst out. "I think you mean you are in a good mood; you're working on motorcycles. Otherwise, you're a grump who is looking for a way to get back in the shop."

"I may slightly resemble that, but you can't be mad at me for knowing what I like and taking it."

"Is that what you are going to call it?" I bumped my shoulder into his. "Sounds better than just being a grump, huh?"

"Careful there, Holly. I might end up letting you know what else I want." His eyes connected with mine, and my breath caught.

"Oh?" I whimpered. What else did Rook want besides working on motorcycles? That was all the man had loved the whole time I'd known him.

He turned toward me and trailed his fingers down my cheek. "We should get back to the trees, sugar, or we are going to be here all night."

Rook stepped back and moved back over to the trees.

Wait, WHAT? The man was going to say that he wanted something else, but then not tell me what that was? Be all flirty, and then tell me we needed to get back to work?

No.

"Hold up," I called. "You better not touch that tree until you tell me what it is you want."

Rook chuckled and shook his head. "Already touched the tree, sugar, so let's just get back to work, yeah?"

I marched over to Rook and stood in front of him. I put my hands on my hips and tipped my head back to look him in the eye. "Tell me what you want," I demanded.

Rook shook his head.

"Yes," I demanded. "What do you want?" I wasn't going to do this weird, awkward dance with Rook.

We had both been teasing and flirting with each other, or at least it seemed like we were to me, and I was going to get to the bottom of this.

"Holly," Rook growled.

"Rook," I replied.

"You have about ten seconds to forget this whole conversation, and we just get back to work."

"And what happens after ten seconds?" I asked.

"Things will change," he motioned between the two of us, "between you and me."

"What if I told you what I want?" I countered. "Then will you tell me what you want?" I was pretty sure we wanted the same thing, but there might be a chance that Rook was being friendly, and I was taking it another way.

"You told me you want a floating tree, sugar. The only thing that is going to do is make more work for me." Rook stepped back, and I stepped toward him.

"I want something more than that."

"Two floating trees?" he laughed.

This was the weird awkwardness I didn't want between us. I was a grown woman who knew what she wanted (even though I had just figured it out), and I was going to take it. Well, I was going to take it if Rook was into me. I wasn't going to throw myself at him and not take no for an answer. There were laws against that.

"No."

"Holly." Rook's voice was stern and low.

"What are you afraid of?" I asked softly.

"A lot of things, Holly. One of them is losing you. We cross the line between us; it doesn't work out, then we lose each other."

"You wouldn't lose me," I replied. I raised my hand and cupped Rook's bearded face. "Kiss me?"

"God damn, Holly," he groaned.

"Please?" I pleaded. "One kiss won't change everything." Even I knew that was a lie.

"Tell me the thing you want," he countered.

A smile spread across my lips. "I just did."

*

Rook

I wanted to kiss Holly, but I also knew everything was going to change when I did. There was no way that things weren't going to.

My heart told me the change would be amazing, but my head also knew if shit went south between the two of us, I would lose Holly completely.

"Rook," she pleaded softly.

Screw it.

We were both adults, and whatever happened, happened.

I delved my fingers into her hair, tipped her head back, and devoured her lips. She moaned into my mouth and wrapped her arms around my shoulders. Her body melded against mine, and it felt like she was made for me.

"Wow," she gasped when we came up for air.

Wow was fucking right. There was a small part of me that had been afraid to kiss Holly because it might not be good.

Thank god that wasn't true.

"Damn, sugar." Calling her sugar was accurate as fuck. She was sweet and tasted delicious: just like sugar. "That was even better than I imagined."

"You imagined what it would be like to kiss me?" she whispered.

"Every damn night since you said you were going to snag one of the bikers who walk through the door."

She wrinkled her nose and shook her head. "I was just kidding."

I tucked her hair behind her ear. "Well, even if you weren't, I can tell you I'm the only biker you're going to be kissing now."

"Is that so?" she asked coyly.

It was the damn truth. I wasn't about to share Holly with anyone. Not if she was with me. "Yes, sugar."

She reached up on her tiptoes and pressed a quick kiss to my lips. "Good answer. Now let's get back to building trees."

"She lures me in like a siren, and then she puts me to work," I grunted.

"How about for every tree we put together, we get a kiss break?" she suggested.

I wrapped my arms around her waist and pulled her body against mine. "Or how about I kiss you whenever I feel like it?"

She licked her lips and sighed. "That sounds even better."

*

Chapter Ten

Holly

"Holly!"

Uh, oh. It was never good when Rook hollered for me from his office.

It had been a week since our night of putting together Christmas trees and discovering we both wanted each other.

It had been downright amazing the past week, and it showed no signs of changing.

Rook and I had agreed that we weren't going to flaunt what was going on between us around the office, but that didn't mean I wasn't taking quick breaks in his office or going to his place when the workday was over.

"Holly," he shouted again.

I jumped up and opened his door. "What's wrong?" I asked.

Rook sat behind his desk and glared as he looked back and forth between his two computer screens. "I can't find it," he grumbled.

I tipped my head to the side. "Find what?" I asked. Rook was a bit tech challenged, but he never seemed to have many problems with his computer.

He had one monitor he used for browsing the web and answering emails, and on the other screen, he kept up the website where he ordered parts.

Rook held up his mouse and shook it. "This damn thing on either of my screens! It's gone!"

A laugh erupted from my lips, and I slapped my hand over my mouth.

"Funny?" he asked. "It won't be too funny when I can't approve the paychecks because I can't find my mouse."

"Dramatic much?" I laughed. I moved around his desk, grabbed the mouse from his hand, and set it down. "Let me have a look."

I moved the mouse around the pad on his desk but couldn't see it either. I clicked it a few times, but still nothing. "Did you try restarting it?" I asked.

"How the heck do I do that when I don't have a mouse?" he grumbled.

I glanced at him over my shoulder, ready to laugh, but the look he gave me strangled the laugh in my throat. "Uh, you can hold down the power button, and it should restart." I kneeled under his desk and held the power button on the computer. "I'm sure it's just a fluke." Most things were fixed by turning it off and then back on.

"Fluke," Rook scoffed. "They tell me this thing is smarter than me, but yet it can't keep my mouse on the screen."

I looked up at him and tried not to smile. "Having a bad day?" I asked.

"The parts I need for the soft tail are on back order, and the exhaust for the Henderson bike isn't fitting," he complained. "It seems if it can go wrong, today it will."

"How long did it say the parts are on backorder for?"

"A week," Rook grumbled. "Which really isn't that long, but I'd like to get started on the bike."

"What about the exhaust?"

Rook leaned back in his chair and sighed. "Dane said he can make it work, but it would just be easier if the shit would go on the way it should."

"Look at your screen," I ordered.

"It's on."

I rolled my eyes. "Move your mouse, Rook. Is it there?"

He moved the mouse, and a small smile spread across his lips. "Thank fuck. It's back."

"You're welcome."

Rook looked down at me and finally gave me one of his panty-dropping smiles. "I guess I just needed you to make things better."

"Well, it has been over three hours since I came in here."

Rook reached out his hand to me, and he pulled me into his lap. He pressed a kiss to my lips and sighed. "Sorry for yelling."

I shrugged and ran my fingers through his beard. "You're forgiven. At least they were easy fixes."

"Everything going okay for you?" he asked softly.

I nodded and traced the bow of his lips. "Confirmed everything with Surly Kabob, finalized the desserts with Mack's Cakes, and the last of the garland should be delivered today."

"Bar and DJ?" he asked.

"Both confirmed. I gave the DJ the list of song suggestions for the bike reveal, and the bartender said the bar would be delivered and set up the day before the reveal."

"You've got everything covered, sugar."

I shrugged and preened a little under his praise. "I try." Things had changed between Rook and me, but it was a change for the better.

"Is the tree still floating by the stairs?" Rook asked.

"Well, I think so. Dane and Trevor haven't yelled about it falling on them yet, so think whatever you did is working."

Rook chuckled, and his body shook beneath me. I laid a hand on his chest and sighed.

It was crazy the way I noticed every little thing about him now. The way he laughed, and his eyes lit with amusement. Or the way his shoulders stretched the fabric of his shirt, and it made my fingers itch to just take the damn thing off.

Hell, Rook just breathing made me want to rip his clothes off.

"What are you thinking about, sugar?" he asked.

My cheeks heated, and my hand moved to the collar of his shirt. "Nothing." I stretched the collar down and caught a glimpse of a black tattoo.

"Sugar," he growled.

"Hmm?" I hummed. I quirked my lips to the side and tried to make out what the tattoo was.

"What are you doing?" he laughed. "You look like you're trying to solve some huge mystery."

"Well," I giggled. "It is sort of a mystery to me. I'm trying to figure out what your tattoo is."

"You're about to rip my shirt if you keep tugging at it like that."

"Just a little bit more," I whispered.

Rook grabbed my hand and pressed a kiss to the palm. "Just take my shirt off, sugar."

My eyes snapped to his. "Rook," I hissed. "We're at work."

"When aren't we?" he chuckled. He moved his arm from around me and nodded to the door. "Lock it."

I glanced at the door and jumped out of his lap. "Don't have to tell me twice," I giggled. I turned the lock on the door and climbed back into his lap.

I tugged up the hem of his shirt and pulled it over his head. I tossed it over my head and heard it hit the floor. "That's better." "Wings." I traced the wings on his chest with my finger, and a smile played on my lips.

"Got 'em when I was young," Rook grunted.

I glanced up at him. "You're still young."

"You're the young one, sugar."

I rolled my eyes. "I'm thirty, Rook, and you're thirty-seven. It's not like there are decades between us or something."

"I just called you in here to find my mouse, Holly," he reminded me.

I giggled and kissed the tip of one of the wings. "Could happen to anyone."

"I'll let you be delusional and not remind you about the grocery delivery five years ago."

"Doesn't make you old," I sighed, "just means you're not into techy stuff."

"You're gonna be good for my ego, Holly." He threaded his fingers through my hair and pulled me close. "Kiss me, sugar. You're exactly what I need to make this day better."

"How did we get here, Rook?" I asked.

"No fucking clue, sugar."

"I'm your secretary."

Rook shook his head. "You're a whole hell of a lot more than that, Holly. Always have been. It just took me five years to see what was right in front of me." His lips crushed my mouth, and his tongue danced with mine.

My hands roamed over his chest, and a growl rumbled from his chest. "We need to stop if you don't want me to lay you out on my desk and have my way with you, Holly," he warned.

"Is that supposed to scare me?" I purred. I pressed a kiss to his collarbone, and my tongue traced the curve of the wing on his chest. "I just locked the door, Rook. It's just you and me in here."

"God dammit, Holly," he growled.

I wanted him, and I wasn't going to run away. "Are you going to make me count to ten before you spread me out on your desk?" I whispered. "One, two, three, fo–."

I didn't get to five before Rook stood with me in his arms and sat me on the edge of his desk. "I'm not playing with you, sugar. Every one of your kisses set me on fire, and I'm on the edge of combusting right here."

I wound my arms around his shoulders and spread my legs for him to stand between. "Sounds good to me." My fingers fumbled with the button of his jeans, but I managed to pop it open.

"Slow down, sugar," he chuckled. "I'm gonna be naked while you have all your clothes on."

That didn't seem bad to me. Finally, seeing Rook was no clothes on was pure heaven.

He pulled my hands off his zipper and kissed my lips. He grabbed the bottom of my Rooks on First t-shirt and pulled it over my head. "Now we're getting somewhere." His eyes darkened, and his fingers went to the clasp of my bra.

For a split second, my mind panicked, knowing I was about to be butt naked on Rook's desk while everyone worked just down the stairs.

"What's wrong?" Rook asked.

"I just realized I'm about to be naked on your desk while everyone else works." Wowzers. I never imagined this would ever happen, but here I was.

"Is that a problem for you?" he asked.

I tipped my head to the side and shrugged. "Well, no. It's not like they are going to know what we're doing."

"Well, they won't as long as you're not a screamer."

I opened my mouth but shut it instantly.

"Oh, sugar," Rook laughed. "This is going to be fun."

*

Rook

Holly leaned back on her elbows, and I scooted her ass to the edge of the desk. I parted the lips of her pussy, and swiped my tongue through her sweet juices.

She was proving that she really was a screamer.

"Oh my god," she moaned. She delved her fingers into my hair and held my head to her pussy.

Holly on my desk was an even better sight than I imagined. Her body was lush and curvy, and my fingers itched to touch every inch of her.

My tongue swirled and teased her tight bud while my hand plunged in and out of her tight hole.

"Don't stop," she pleaded.

My tongue moved faster, and she bucked her hips up to meet my mouth.

Her orgasm washed over her, and she screamed my name. We were upstairs, and everyone was working downstairs, but I would be surprised if we didn't get a few knowing glances when we got back to work.

"More," Holly gasped. "I need more of you."

"You're fucking insatiable, sugar." I wiped my mouth with the back of my hand and looked down at her spread out before me like a feast.

My dick was rock hard, and I couldn't wait another second to make Holly mine.

I lined my dick up with the entrance of her pussy and pushed inside her. "God damn," I growled. Holly's pussy squeezed my dick like a damn vice, and I closed my eyes to restrain myself from coming instantly.

"Are you okay?" Holly whispered.

My eyes snapped open, and Holly looked at me like she had done something wrong.

"You're fucking tight, sugar. I'm trying not to go off like a fucking rocket ten seconds in," I ground out. My dick was planted deep inside her, and I felt the walls of her pussy flex around me.

"Does that help?" she asked coyly.

"Woman," I hissed. "You do that again, and this is going to be over before it even starts."

She smiled slyly, and she squeezed me again.

I grabbed her by the back of the neck and hauled her off the desk until her chest was flush against me. "You're a fucking vixen, sugar. You're trying to torture me."

"Maybe," she whispered.

"Two can play that game." I slowly pulled out and plunged back into her.

"Again," she pleaded. "More." Her hands roamed over my body as her pussy milked my cock with each thrust of my hips.

I tried to hold back the tidal wave that threatened to take me under, but Holly's tight pussy drained my balls after only a few minutes.

I collapsed on top of her, and she wrapped her arms around me.

"I think this is a great way to unwind from a stressful workday," Holly sighed.

"You were stressed, sugar?" I mumbled into her hair.

She laughed lightly. "Well, no, but you were. I'm totally fine with you working out your stress with me."

"As long as I'm the only one you're offering those services to, sugar."

"You're all I want, Rook. The biker I didn't know I needed."

I pressed a soft kiss to her lips and sighed.

"We need to get cleaned up and answer your phone that keeps ringing."

Holly's head snapped up, and she tipped it to the side. "I didn't even hear it ringing," she laughed.

I helped her off my desk and set her on her feet. "That means I did a good job."

She playfully slapped my chest and laughed. "Your ego doesn't need any more boosting."

I grabbed her shirt from by the door and tossed it to her. "You're coming home with me tonight."

"Is that a question or an order?" She grabbed her bra from the back of the chair and looped her arms through it.

"Whichever one is going to guarantee we spend all night in my bed." I slipped on my boxers and looked around for my pants.

"They're under your desk," Holly laughed. She fastened her bra and pulled her shirt on. "To be honest, question or demand, I'll be in your bed."

I grabbed her around the waist and pulled her into my arms.

"Rook," she laughed, "you just told me we have to get back to work."

"I know," I growled. "I can't seem to keep my hands off of you."

She rolled her eyes and pressed a kiss to my lips. "The feeling is mutual, but we really do need to get to work."

"Yeah, yeah," I grumbled. For once, I didn't want to go build shit in the garage. I would have preferred to spend all day locked in my office with Holly.

Now, that was something I didn't see coming.

*

Chapter Eleven

Holly

Everything was set.

Tomorrow was the Christmas bike reveal for the Henderson's, and Rooks on First looked like a winter wonderland with a biker twist.

All the bikes on the showroom floor were draped with garland and lights, and there were six trees around the perimeter of the showroom. The bar was set up by the service desk, and there were two long tables draped with snow-white table clothes where the food would be tomorrow.

The shop had six total trees in the area, including one floating from the stairs to the offices. Lights were strung all around, and Rook even helped me decorate the toolboxes with lights and ornaments.

Rook may have started out hating the idea of a Christmas bike reveal, but he was helping way more than I thought he would.

"Holly."

I spun around on my heel and smiled when Rook stood in the doorway to the showroom.

"Hi," I smiled. Rook had taken the Henderson bike for one final test drive, and I hoped everything was okay. "Did the bike run good?"

Rook nodded and motioned for me to follow him.

I took one last look around the shop and headed into the showroom.

My breath caught, and I clutched my hand to my chest. "Oh my god."

In the center of the showroom was a vast, twelve-foot Christmas tree with thousands of lights shining brightly.

"You like it?" Rook asked.

I slowly walked around the tree and nodded. "It is beautiful, Rook. When on earth did you do this?"

Rook shrugged and leaned against the bar. "While I took the Henderson bike for a test ride, Dane and the rest of the guys set up the tree."

I felt the branches and smiled.

"I sprung for the one that was easy assembly."

"I'm not sure that was in the budget," I teased.

"Fuck the budget if it means I get to see you smile like that."

"Rook," I sighed. "Don't be so sweet to me."

Rook shrugged and pushed off the bar. "Just saying the truth, sugar."

I stepped back and gazed up at the tree.

Rook wrapped his arms around me from behind and pressed a kiss to my neck. "Merry Christmas, sugar."

I sighed and relaxed in his arms. "It is with you, Rook." I quirked my eyebrow and smiled. "Have you ever had sex beneath a Christmas tree before?" I laughed.

Rook spun me around in his arms. "Have you?" he countered.

I bit my bottom lip and shook my head.

"Looks like we're both gonna mark that one off our list tonight, sugar."

*

Chapter Twelve

Rook

I don't know how, but Holly had done it.

Christmas was not my thing, but even I had to admit Rooks on First looked absolutely stunning.

So far, it seemed everyone was having an amazing time.

Even Mindy, who got almost nothing she had asked for, seemed to be basking in all her friends telling her how amazing everything was.

Of course, she was omitting the fact she had done absolutely nothing and took all the credit.

Holly had been flitting around the past hour, ensuring all the food was perfect. I had managed to corner her in my office before the party started and told her exactly what I thought about her tight black jeans and deep red blouse.

I caught a glimpse of her over by the bar and headed that direction. I had just passed the giant tree we had made love under last night when someone grabbed my hand and called my name.

"Rook."

I knew that voice.

I hadn't heard it in a year when the last thing that had told me was I wouldn't be anything more than a biker.

"Monica," I gritted out between clenched teeth. She was the last person I wanted to see tonight.

Monica and I had dated for a couple of months last year, but things hadn't worked out when she made it clear that I wasn't up to her standards.

"I hope you don't mind that I'm here. Mindy and I know each other from the clubhouse, and she mentioned last minute that she was having a little party here."

I nodded and glanced in the direction of Holly.

Holly had met Monica before, and she knew we had dated.

Holly was talking to the bartender, but her eyes darted to me.

Fuck.

Monica reached out and laid her hand on my arm. "I have to say, Rook, I'm amazed at how well you are doing."

Monica was always good at backhanded compliments. "Business has been steady for about five years, Monica."

She tipped her head to the side. "Oh, really? I had no idea when we were dating."

That's because I hadn't flaunted my money in her face and bought her expensive presents. She had been to the shop twice before, and it wasn't impressive to her. I was a guy who had dirty hands and built motorcycles. Not her type.

I didn't reply because I didn't want to give Monica any more of my time.

She moved closer to me and beamed up at me. "I must admit, I came tonight because I wanted to tell you I've missed you."

Bull. Shit.

Monica had come tonight because she wanted to affirm that she had made the right decision a year ago.

She hadn't, but I was the one who had dodged a bullet.

I would have been miserable with her greedy ass, and I would have missed out on Holly.

Mindy clinked a knife to her wine glass and called for everyone to quiet down.

"Rook," Monica called. She leaned even closer, and I felt her breath against my face. "I think we need to talk."

I shook her off my arm and glared at her. "We don't have shit to talk about, Monica. I haven't

thought about you in over a year. Have a good life."
I turned on my heel and headed straight for Holly.

She had, of course, seen the whole scene with Monica, and I prayed to god she wasn't going to make a big deal about it. But to be honest, I would understand if she did; I just hoped she listened to me when I told her it was nothing.

Mindy and Mitch were both droning on about how grateful they were for their amazing friends and how much they loved all of them, but I barely heard a word of it.

Holly had her arms folded over her chest and a frown on her lips. I stopped in front of her and racked my brain for the right thing to say.

"Monica?" she asked.

I nodded.

"She wasn't on the guest list."

"She said Mindy invited her last minute."

Holly hmphed, and her eyes stayed on me. "What did she have to say?"

"Said she missed me."

Holly nodded. "And what did you say to her?"

"Told her I hadn't thought about her since the day she told me I wasn't good enough for her."

"That must be when her eyes bugged out of her head."

I chuckled and ran my fingers through my hair.

"Do you want to be with me, Rook?" Holly asked, point blank.

"Yeah." I didn't even have to think about it. Holly was what I wanted. She was it.

Holly nodded. "Good."

"You want to be with me?" I asked.

She shrugged, but a smile spread across her lips. "I suppose. You're kind of out of my league, but that's your problem, not mine."

I grabbed her around the waist and hauled her into my arms.

"Rook," she gasped. Her eyes darted around the room, and she tried to pull out of my arms.

"No, Holly," I whispered. I pressed a kiss to her lips and felt her relax in my arms. "I'm not hiding you from anyone. I'm yours, and everyone is going to know it."

"Even everyone who works for you?" she whispered.

I didn't have the heart to tell her that pretty much everyone already knew. That day we had broken in my desk, she had been loud, and Dane and a couple of other guys happened to be in the breakroom.

"You trying to hide the fact you're banging the boss?" I laughed.

Holly rolled her eyes and slapped my chest. "You're crazy, Rook."

I spotted a flash of red, and my eyes snapped to a Santa Clause in red pants and a black leather vest. "I think you might be right. Is that Santa?"

Holly laughed and nodded. "That's Megan's dad. I asked him if he could be biker Santa for the night."

"That's fucking hilarious, sugar." And it looked like everyone loved it. Hell, I loved it.

"And cheap. He's good with free booze and food." Holly winked and pressed a kiss to my cheek.

"Even better."

And that's how everything was with Holly around.

Better.

"And now, let's see the bike!" Mindy called.

"Fuck," I hissed. That was my cue to crank up the bike and pull it into the showroom.

The bike roared to life, and the crowd around the tree parted to watch Dane pull the bike up to Mitch and Mindy.

"I covered for you," Holly called. She cupped my cheek, and I turned my head to look at her. "Dane was at the bar when you were talking to Monica, and I asked him to pull out the bike because you had your hands full."

I grumbled and tightly wrapped my arms around her waist. "Thank you, sugar. You always have my back."

Holly shrugged. "I try."

Everyone was clamoring to get closer to the bike, but Holly and I were in our own world.

"What was it I promised you if you managed to pull off this party?" I asked.

Holly smirked and unbuttoned the top button of my shirt. "I believe it was two tickets for a seven-day cruise."

"Two tickets?" I asked. "What are you going to do with two tickets?"

She unbuttoned another button. "I know a biker who I think would want to come, but he's a workaholic. I don't know if he'll want to come."

"Oh yeah?"

She tipped her head back and nodded. "I might have to convince him to come."

"Nah," I chuckled. "I think all you're gonna have to do is ask him. He'd be a fool to say no."

Holly leaned up on her tiptoes and pressed a kiss to my lips. "Run away with me for seven days, biker?"

I swept her up in my arms, and she wrapped her arms around my neck. "You got it, sugar. I'm yours."

*

Chapter Thirteen

Holly

"Hello?" Minx called.

I stood on the landing of the stairs to the offices and watched Rook make small talk with people from the party.

"Minx?" I laughed.

"Girl, what are you calling me for? I thought you had your big party tonight," she asked.

"I do, but I just had to call and tell you something."

"Um, okay?" Minx giggled.

I took a deep breath and smiled when Rook looked up at me. "I got my biker."

*

Coming Soon

Jinx
Roya Bastards MC
Book 7

About the Author

Wall Street Journal and USA Today bestselling author Winter Travers is a devoted wife, mother, and aunt-turned-author who was born and raised in Wisconsin. After a brief stint in South Carolina, following her heart to chase the man who is now her hubby, they retreated back up North to the changing seasons and to the place they now call home.

Winter spends her days writing happily-ever-afters and her nights being a karate mom hauling her son to practices and tournaments. She also has an addiction to anything MC-related, puppies and baking.

Winter loves to stay connected with her readers. Don't hesitate to reach out and contact her.

Facebook

Twitter

Instagram

Website

Mailing List

Goodreads

BookBub

Check out the first chapter of Wilder Presley
Says He Loves Me

Chapter One

He's back...

Shelby

"He's back."

I snagged the last roll of black ribbon and dropped it into my basket.

"I saw him this morning at the diner. When he walked right by, I was getting my two scrambled eggs with wheat toast and maple sausage." Missy clicked her tongue. "He looked as fine as fireworks on the fourth of July out on Mason Lake, let me tell you."

My eyes searched the shelf for the second time hoping for black ribbon to magically appear. "Maybe they have more black ribbon in the back," I mumbled. I needed at least five more yards to ensure I had enough to finish the wreath Mrs. Baxter ordered. Halloween was fast approaching, and I needed to get a jump on my standing orders.

"Shelby Lyn." Missy snapped her fingers in my face. "Have you heard a word I've said?"

I stepped back and swatted her hand out of my face. "Yeah, you ate your breakfast this morning, and it was as good as the fourth of July fireworks."

Missy scoffed. "You missed the important part."

Missy spoke a mile a minute, and while I'm sure most of what she said was necessary to someone somewhere, most of the time, I tuned her out. After almost twenty years of friendship, I learned that if I missed something important that came out of her mouth, she tended to return to it until I heard her. This was one of those times. "Then tell me the important part while we wait for Jack to get his ass out of the backroom and help me."

"You know he's probably reading the old *Playboys* back there." Missy visibly shivered. "Thank god I never had a boy. I don't think I could have handled the crusty socks and forty-minute showers."

"Missy. Did you need to go there?" Dear god in heaven. I did not need that mental picture painted in my brain. "I doubt Jack is doing anything in the backroom. Please, he's eighteen. I hope he can control himself till he gets off work."

Missy shrugged. "Girl, you remember how boys were when we were eighteen. Horn dogs looking to rut."

"Uh, rut?" Was she talking about men or deer? *Sometimes the lines did blur.*

She scoffed and grabbed the dark blue ribbon. "Dad was watching the hunting channel last time I stopped by. What about this one?"

I shook my head. "It's navy."

"Nonsense. This is black," she insisted.

I grabbed the ribbon from her and set it back on the shelf. "It's navy, and it won't work." The backroom door swung open, and Jack walked out. "There's Jack."

"Oh lordy. See, he's tucking his shirt in." Missy hissed. "Whatever you do, do not touch his hands," she advised.

"Jack," I called. "Can you check to see if there is any more one-inch black ribbon in the back?"

Jack gave me a two-fingered salute and backtracked to the backroom.

"Gonna be ten minutes before he surfaces again. You gave him an excuse to read a few more pages," Missy laughed.

"You're a nut, Missy." I moved over to the selection of orange ribbons and tried to figure out which shade would be perfect. It needed to be bright, but not neon bright.

"Can we get back to what we were talking about before?"

"Your breakfast? It must have been pretty good if you want to keep talking about it." I fingered a light shade of orange and wondered if it would clash with the dark shadow of orange I already had at home. Mrs. Baxter was as sweet as pie, but she would have a bird if the colors weren't right for her fall wreath.

Missy scoffed. "Wilder Presley is back, Shelby," she shouted.

I dropped the light orange ribbon, and Missy's words hit me like bullets to my head. "Uh, what?" There was no way she had just said *that*.

No.

No, no, no.

Missy snapped her fingers in my face. "Now you're gonna listen, huh?" she laughed. She shook her head and turned to the rack of ribbon. "What if you did a dark purple instead of black?" she suggested.

I grabbed her shoulder and spun her back to face me. "We're not going to talk about ribbon right now," I spat.

"You're about a minute behind on your shock, Shelby. I'm over having to tell you about Wilder."

"I was listening all along," I muttered.

"Wilder Presley is back in Adams, Shelby Lyn, and you look like you saw a ghost."

I glared at Missy. "I heard you the first time you said it."

Missy cackled. "Second time I said it, you heard, but I had to repeat it because the look you get when I say his name says so much."

I didn't get a look when she said his name. There was no reason why I would get a look. *None.* "Where is Jack with my ribbon?" I grumbled.

"So you're just going to act like I didn't tell you *the* Wilder Presley is home?" Missy smirked. "You can't act like this with me, Shelby." She wagged her finger in my face. "I have known you for nineteen years and one hundred ten days.

I rolled my eyes. I wasn't acting anyway, just like I hadn't had a look when she said Wilder's name. "And this isn't his home," I insisted. "When you leave for more than ten years, the place you go to becomes your home."

"Is that a rule?" Missy questioned.

"Here ya go," Jack called. He held up three rolls of black ribbon. "These are the last of them." He made his way to me, and I grabbed the rolls from him.

"Thanks." I nodded to the orange ribbon. "I need to grab a couple of rolls of orange. I'll meet you at the register."

Jack nodded. "Sounds good."

I grabbed two shades of orange and hoped they would work for the wreath, but my mind was too wound up about Wilder to even notice what I grabbed.

"Shelby," Missy called.

My eyes darted to her. "What?"

"What is going on in that head of yours right now?" she demanded.

I shrugged and dropped the orange ribbon into my basket. "I think I have two days to finish this wreath, and then I need to start thinking about the Christmas wreaths for the church while I work on the twenty other orders I have for fall or Halloween wreaths. I'm busy, Missy."

Missy tipped her head to the side and crossed her arms over her chest. "You are so full of shit, girlfriend. The man you had a crush on all of your life is back in town, and you're going to tell me you're thinking about wreaths?"

I nodded my head. "Yes, you will believe that because you are my best friend, and you know I don't want to have this conversation at the craft store." I turned on my heel and headed to where Jack stood behind the check-out counter.

"You know I'm just going to come over to your house after I get off of work," Missy called after me.

I raised my hand over my head. "I wouldn't expect anything less from you, Missy." Missy had been my best friend for almost twenty years. She had moved to Adams when we were both ten and had become one of my close friends that summer.

"You want wine or hard booze?" she asked.

I needed a damn tranquilizer if what she had told me was true. "Bring the Southern," I replied.

"Woo, wee," Missy chuckled. "This is going to be a fun night."

I rolled my eyes and set my basket on the check-out counter. "You wouldn't by chance, have a bottle of booze behind the counter, would you, Jack?" I blew my hair out of my face and sighed.

"Uh, well, I think my dad might have a bottle hidden in his office," Jack stammered. "I could see if I could get you a glass."

Oh, sweet Jack. He was just a little too naïve for his good.

I nodded to the basket. "I think I can make it home without a glass. Thank you, though."

Jack looked visibly relieved.

Five minutes later, I was sitting behind the steering wheel of my truck and closed my eyes.

Wilder Presley was back in town.

Twelve years ago, I had watched that man drive out of my life with not so much as a backward glance. He had broken my heart that day, and I hadn't even known it.

Wilder Presley was back, and so were all those feelings I thought I had buried.

No amount of Southern was going to make this any easier.

*